A Birthday Bike for Brimhall

A Birthday Bike for Brimhall

by Judy Delton
pictures by June Leary

A Young Yearling Book

Published by
Dell Publishing
a division of
Bantam Doubleday Dell Publishing Group, Inc.
666 Fifth Avenue
New York, New York 10103

ISBN: 0-440-40461-4

Reprinted by arrangement with Carolrhoda Books, Inc.

Printed in the United States of America

May 1991

10 9 8 7 6 5 4 3 2 1

WES

For Jack and Maura Minogue, the best neighbors
a writer could have
J.D.

To those who grin and bear with me
J.L.

Contents

HAPPY BIRTHDAY BRIMHALL!

Chapter One

Brimhall had saved
his biggest birthday present
for last.
It was from Roger.
Brimhall knew that it would be
something special.
He took his time untying the bow.
He removed the paper very carefully.

"Oh, my!" he cried.

"Do you like it, Brimhall?

Do you like it?" asked Roger.

"Why...ah...yes, Roger.

It is a very fine bike."

Brimhall ran his hand
along the shiny red fender.
"It is a *beautiful* bike," said Bear.
Roger hopped up and down.
"Let's take it outside and try it out!"

"Brimhall should ride first," said Bear.

"It is his birthday."

"And it's his bike," added Roger.

"No, no."

Brimhall waved a paw generously.

"You go first, Bear."

Bear rode off down the garden path.

"Whee!" he called

as he pedaled toward the rose bush.

When he came around it

his feet were up on the handlebars.

"Look, no hands!" he shouted

as he coasted back to them.

"It's Brimhall's turn now," said Roger.

"Er...you go next, Roger,"
said Brimhall.
"I have a cramp in my knee."
He shook his leg
and danced around in a circle,
rubbing his knee.

Roger frowned. "Well, all right.
But just a short spin."
The bike was large for a rabbit,
but Roger stretched his legs.
Up and down the garden path
he zoomed.

"You will really enjoy this, Brimhall,"
he said as he climbed off.
"And it will be good exercise for you.
You are a large bear, you know.
Exercise will keep you in shape."
Brimhall frowned.
"I am in fine shape, Roger."
"Well," said Roger quickly,
"the bike will be good
for going shopping.
Try it out, Brimhall.
I'll hold it while you get on."
"Er...it's getting dark, Roger.
I think I'd better wait till morning
when it is good and light.
Yes, that's it.
When the sun is shining brightly."

Bear and Roger looked at the sky.
"Brimhall, the sun *is* shining brightly,"
said Bear.

"It will be shining better
tomorrow morning," said Brimhall,
and he took his bike inside.

17

Chapter Two

That evening Bear fixed supper.
Brimhall polished his bike.
He leaned it against his bedroom wall
and looked at it.
Then he closed the door.
"I don't even know how
to get on a bike," he muttered.

Finally he got himself onto the seat.
He put his feet carefully on the pedals
and pushed away from the wall.
The front wheel weaved
back and forth.
Brimhall ran into his bureau
and fell to the floor with a crash.
The bike fell on top of him.
Bear ran into the bedroom.
"Brimhall, are you hurt?
What happened?"
"Er...nothing, Bear," said Brimhall.
"Nothing at all.
I was just polishing my bike,
and it fell over."
"Well, come along and have supper
now," said Bear.

Brimhall stood the bike
back against the wall.
Then he followed Bear to the kitchen.
He gave the bike a little kick
before he left his room.

The next morning
Roger came by bright and early.
"Brimhall?" he called.
"Are you ready to ride your new bike?"
Brimhall came to the door.
He was still in his pajamas.
"It looks like rain, Roger.
I don't want to take my new bike
out in the rain."
"It's as dry as can be, Brimhall,"
said Roger.
"I can't take any chances,"
said Brimhall. "Rust.
That's the worst thing for a bike.
It makes the gears stiff.
No, sir.
I'll just have to wait
until I'm positively sure
that it won't rain."

"Brimhall?"
called Bear a little later.
"Are you going to take your bike out
this morning?"
Bike, bike, bike.
Brimhall was beginning to hate
the sound of the word.
"Rust!" he answered.
"Rust could ruin a bike, Bear."

"You could ride to the market,"
said Bear.
"We could use some greens for dinner."
"We don't need greens for dinner,"
said Brimhall crossly.
"Just make dinner without greens."
"I'll go myself, then," said Bear.
When he was sure that Bear had gone,
Brimhall went outside.
He looked up and down the path.
He didn't see anyone.

Brimhall got his bike.

"Now, Brimhall," he said to himself,
"there is no reason to be afraid.
If Bear and Roger can ride,
you can ride."

Brimhall put one foot on one pedal.
He put his other foot
on the other pedal.
He began to move.
The front wheel wobbled
from one side of the path
to the other.
The more Brimhall tried
to steer one way,
the more the bike
went the other way.
Suddenly it hit a stone.
Over it fell, right into the stream,
with Brimhall on top of it.

NO FISHING

"I will never be able to ride this bike,"
Brimhall grumbled.
He got up and wiped the mud
from his suit.
"My poor bike," he moaned.
"Full of mud, just like me."

Brimhall pushed his bike home.
His knee was skinned.
His elbow ached.

30

He washed off his bike.
Then he changed his clothes
and lay down on his bed to think.

31

From his bed
all he could see was the red bike.
He moved to a chair
on the other side of the room,
but he could still see the bike.
Brimhall took a blanket from his bed.
He put it over the bike.
"I don't want to see you
for a long, long time,"
he growled.

Chapter Three

The next morning
Roger was at the door again.
Brimhall was wearing dark glasses.
"I can't see, Roger," he said
as he felt his way out the front door.
"A terrible disease has struck my eyes.
I may never see again."

"Oh, dear!" said Roger.

"Let me take you to the doctor,
Brimhall."

Brimhall held up a paw.

"I've already been to the doctor.
There is only one cure, Roger:
WALKING.
I must walk everywhere I go.
Only on foot, the doctor says."

"That is a shame, Brimhall,"
said Roger.

"I hope you recover soon
so we can go bike riding together."

"It will take some time," said Brimhall
as he felt his way back into the house

When Bear went out for the afternoon,
Brimhall took off his dark glasses.

Then he took the blanket off his bike.

"I *will* learn to ride.

I WILL learn to ride.

I WILL learn to ride,"
he told himself.

Brimhall walked his bike outside.
Then he went to the basement
and got two long poles.
He held one pole in each hand,
like canes.
Then he climbed onto his bike.
He put his feet on the pedals
and balanced himself with the poles.
So far, so good, he thought.
He began to pedal.
"Oh, no!" he shouted
as he crashed into the garden wall.
"I can't steer!"
Brimhall picked himself
and his bike up
and went back to the house.
"My new red bike
is going to be worn-out
before I learn to ride it," he said.

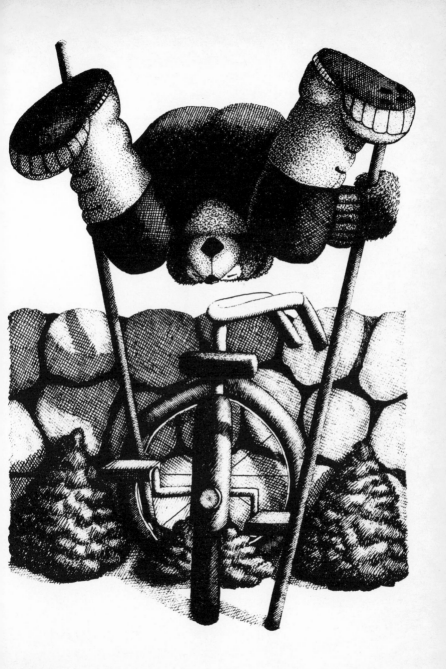

"Training wheels!" said Brimhall,
snapping his fingers.
"I will make a set of training wheels."
Back to the basement he went.
He hammered and he pounded
until he had made
two wooden training wheels.
Brimhall fastened the training wheels
onto his bike
and climbed back up on the seat.
He pedaled slowly down the path.
Before long he was riding!
Faster and faster he pedaled.
Faster and faster went the bike.
"Dear me!" shouted Brimhall.
"I don't remember how to stop!"

Brimhall sailed by the market
and the fish store.
He flew past city hall and the park.

Then one of the training wheels fell off.
Brimhall and the bike
crashed into a rose bush.

Brimhall got up wearily,
pulled the thorns out of his jacket,
and started the long walk home.
"At least I rode a long way
before I fell," he sighed,
"but I'm not sure that it was worth it."

Chapter Four

Every day Roger came
and asked about the bike.
Every day Bear told Brimhall
to take it out for a ride.
And every day
Brimhall hated the bike more.
He wanted to give it back to Roger.
He wanted to roll it off a cliff.
But he didn't want
to hurt Roger's feelings.

One afternoon there was a loud crash.

Brimhall ran to the kitchen.

Bear was lying on the floor.

"Help me, Brimhall!" cried Bear.

"I fell off the chair.

I think my leg is broken."

"I'll get the doctor!" shouted Brimhall.

Then he remembered

how far it was to the doctor's house.

He rushed into his bedroom

and pulled the blanket off his bike.

He rolled it out the front door.

He didn't stop to give himself advice.

He didn't stop to make training wheels.

He jumped onto the bike

and pedaled as fast as he could.

He was all the way to the doctor's house
before he thought about riding a bike!
"Why, I *can* ride a bike!" he shouted.
Brimhall ran
into the doctor's office.
"Come quickly, Doctor.
Bear has broken his leg!"
The doctor grabbed his bag
and followed Brimhall out the door.

"I didn't know you could ride a bike,
Brimhall," said the doctor
when he saw the bike.
"Yes. Yes, I can!" said Brimhall proudly.
"It's not hard, you know."
"Really?" asked the doctor.
He climbed on behind Brimhall.
"You should learn," said Brimhall.
"You could reach your patients
in half the time."
"Perhaps you are right,"
said the doctor.
"But I could never learn to ride a bike."
"I could teach you," Brimhall offered.

Just then they came to Bear's house.

"Why, Brimhall," said Bear,

"how ever did you get back so quickly?"

"I just rode my bike," said Brimhall.

"It's very fast, you know.

And good exercise besides."

The doctor bandaged Bear's leg,

and he and Brimhall

helped Bear to bed.

"It's just a sprain," said the doctor.

"Keep off your foot for a few days,

Bear, and you will be just fine."

That evening Roger came by
for a game of checkers with Bear.
"...and if Brimhall hadn't
had his bike, Roger," said Bear,
"why, I might have had
to lie there in pain for hours."
Roger and Bear looked out the window.
Brimhall was sailing by on his bike.
"Look!" he called. "No hands!"
"How about a game of checkers,
Brimhall?" called Roger.
"No thanks," Brimhall called back.
"I'm on my way to town.
There's a bicycle race tonight, I heard.
I thought I'd go and...er...watch?
By the way, Roger, did I ever thank you
for the birthday present?

It was just exactly what I needed!"